This book belongs to

. . . .

. . . .

LONDON, NEW YORK, DELHI, SYDNEY, PARIS, MUNICH, and JOHANNESBURG

Written in consultation with child psychologist Flora Hogman, Ph.D.

Project Editor Hannah Wilson
Senior Art Editor Sonia Whillock
Senior Editor Linda Esposito
U.S. Editor Beth Sutinis
Production Silvia La Greca
Jacket Design Victoria Harvey

First American Edition, 2001
Published in the United States by DK Publishing, Inc.
95 Madison Avenue, New York, NY 10016

2 4 6 8 10 9 7 5 3 1

Library of Congress Cataloging-in-Publication Data

Robbins, Beth.

Tom's first haircut / by Beth Robbins ; illustrated by Jon Stuart.
    p. cm. -- (It's O.K.)
Summary: Worried about shampoo in his eyes, sharp scissors, and looking silly, Tom the cat
is surprised when he has a fantastic time on his first trip to the hairdresser for a haircut.
ISBN 0-7894-7425-5 -- ISBN 0-7894-7424-7 (pbk.)
[1. Haircutting--Fiction. 2. Fear--Fiction. 3. Cats--Fiction. 4. Animals--Fiction.]
I. Stuart, Jon, ill. II. Title. III. Series.
PZ7.R53235 Ne 2001
[E]--dc21   00-058937

Color reproduction by Colourscan, Singapore
Printed and bound by L.E.G.O. in Italy

see our complete
catalog at
www.dk.com

Tom's New HAIRCUT

IT'S OK!

BY BETH ROBBINS

ILLUSTRATED BY JON STUART

DK Publishing, Inc.

It had rained all week, but now the sun was out.
Tom and Lionel spent all morning playing in the backyard.

5

When they went into the house for a drink,
Tom's mom was a little upset.

"Look at the two of you," she said.
"You look like you went
through a hedge backward!"

"We have," said Tom.
"Twice!" said Lionel.

Mom looked Tom up and down.
"You've been looking a little messy
for a while now," she said.
"It's time you had a real haircut."

"A *real* haircut?" Tom repeated.

He didn't like the sound of that.
Mom sometimes gave him
a little trim, but this sounded serious.

"Won't it hurt?"
asked Tom.

"Of course not!" said Mom.
"It's just time you had a real haircut at a real hairdresser.
They'll do a much better job than I."

"But I like my hair the way it is," wailed Tom.

"My mom said I've got to get
my hair cut, too," said Lionel.
"My grandpa is taking me
to the hairdresser on Saturday morning."

"Can I go with Lionel?" asked Tom.
"Can he?" asked Lionel.
"Then we can have our hair cut together."

Mom smiled. "I'll call
the hairdresser and see."

She made an appointment
for Tom without
any problem at all.

All week, Tom couldn't stop thinking about having his first real haircut.

At first, he was excited. Lionel said it would be an adventure.

But then Ally started teasing Tom. "You'd better watch out for sharp scissors with your sticking-out ears!" she said.

Dad told Ally to stop it.

Then he patted Tom on the head. "In this hot weather, you'll feel much better with short hair."

Tom had to admit he felt hot.

"You'll be as bald as an egg," Ally teased when Mom and Dad weren't around.

On Saturday morning, Lionel and his grandpa came to get Tom.

"We've got plenty of time," said Grandpa, looking at his watch.
"I thought we could take a walk in the park."

"Tell us one of your stories, Grandpa," said Lionel.
"Yes, please!" said Tom.

Lionel's grandpa told great stories. Mom said some of them were "tall." Tom wasn't sure what that meant.

"All right." Grandpa laughed. "I'll tell you the story of my first haircut."

"Oh, no!" thought Tom. He had wanted a story that would take his mind *off* haircuts.

"My story begins when I was a young cub,
not much older than you two," said Grandpa.
"One day, my mom said it was time
I had a real haircut."

"Did you go to the hairdresser?" asked Lionel.
"No," said Grandpa, "I was naughty.
I wouldn't go."

"What did your mom do?" asked Tom.

"Well," said Grandpa, "she tried everything. But when someone doesn't want to do something, it's hard to make them."

"So what happened?" asked Lionel. "I learned that I should have gone to the hairdresser in the first place!" Grandpa chuckled.

"But what *happened*?" pleaded Lionel.

"My hair grew," said Grandpa.
"That's what happened!

"At first I thought
it looked really good.
But it kept on growing,
and growing.
It just wouldn't stop!

"Soon all sorts of critters
were living in it.
They thought I was a tree!
I asked them to leave,
but they didn't listen."

"So, what did you do?"
asked Tom.

"Well." Grandpa chuckled. "I tried to brush them out by walking between two bushes. But my hair got all tangled up.

"My dad had to cut me out with a pair of gardening shears. I ended up with the worst haircut in the world!"

Tom and Lionel were enjoying Grandpa's story so much that they were at the hairdresser before they knew it.

They were a little early.

"Hello," said Mr. Shearer, the owner. "Take a seat over there. You can have a look at the style books while you're waiting."

Mr. Shearer was busy perming a poodle. His assistant stood by his side, handing him little rollers.

Ramsey Shearer was sitting in another seat.
He waved to Tom and Lionel.
"I like my hair really short for the summer,"
he shouted over the hum of the electric clippers.

Mr. Shearer's assistant brought over
three glasses of orange juice.
"Hello, my name's Zeno," he said.
"Mr. Shearer will be ready for you soon."

Tom and Lionel flipped through
the style books while Grandpa
read the newspaper.

Ten minutes later, Zeno came back.
"Follow me, please," he said.
"Mr. Shearer wants me
to wash your hair.
I'll get two plastic smocks."

"I hope they're not like that,"
whispered Lionel.
He pointed to the poodle
who was having her hair permed.
Her smock was covered with flowers.

But they didn't need to worry.
The smocks were blue and had pictures of dinosaurs on them.

Tom thought he looked pretty cool in his.

They followed Zeno to a row of sinks.

Tom didn't want to have his hair washed.
He was worried Zeno would get shampoo in his eyes.

"Who's first?" asked Zeno.
"Tom can go first," said Lionel, as if he were being polite.

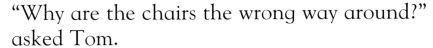

"Why are the chairs the wrong way around?"
asked Tom.
"They're not," laughed Zeno.
"You sit with your back to the sink.
That way I won't get shampoo in your eyes."

Zeno wrapped a towel around Tom's neck.

Then he adjusted the height of the chair, so Tom could comfortably lean his head back over the sink.

Zeno turned on the water spray and tested it on his hand until the temperature was just right.

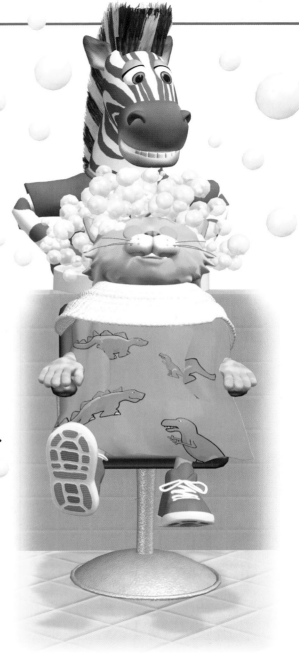

"Is that O.K.?" Zeno asked,
as he wet Tom's head.

Tom nodded.

Zeno put a blob of shampoo
between Tom's ears
and began to work it into a lather.

The shampoo smelled good.

Tom closed his eyes.
This wasn't bad at all.

In fact, it felt really nice.
He had to stop himself
from purring.

Zeno rinsed Tom's hair and wrapped a clean, fluffy towel around his head, then brought him to Mr. Shearer.

Zeno went back to Lionel,
who was now looking forward to his shampoo.

Mr. Shearer was very friendly.
He sat Tom in a big comfy chair.

He swiveled the chair around and around.
It got higher and higher until Tom
could see himself in the mirror.

"Now, young man," said
Mr. Shearer, smiling,
"is there a
special haircut
you would like?"

"Not too short," said Tom.
"And please be careful of my ears!"

"Don't worry, you're in safe hands," said Mr. Shearer, laughing.
"But it would help me if you sat still."

Then he began to snip with his scissors.
Tom watched the snippets of hair
fall all around him.

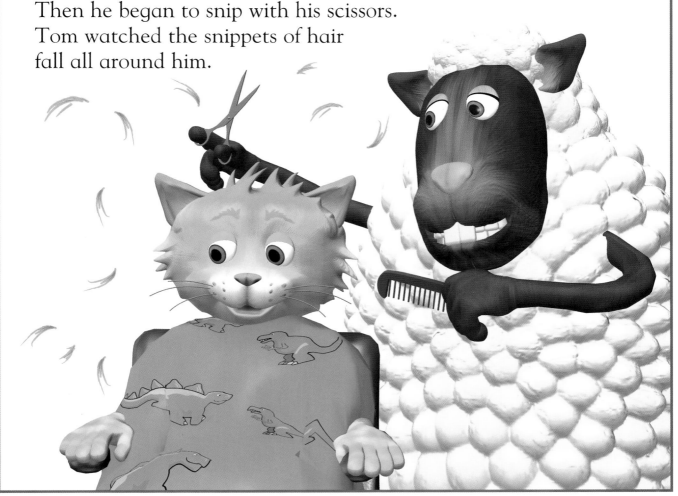

Mr. Shearer finished with a warm blast from the hairdryer

and a tiny slick of styling gel.

"Wow!" cried Lionel. "You look great!"

Tom smiled. He felt very grown up.

"Would you like the same, Lionel?" asked Mr. Shearer.

"Yes, please!" said Lionel.

"You two look so good, I feel scruffy!" said Grandpa, as they left the hairdresser. "Shall we walk home through the park?"

But Tom and Lionel wanted to walk through the shopping mall,

so they could admire their new haircuts in the store windows.